Leslie C. Bennison

Rosemary Mitchell

SUSSEX
A KIPLING ANTHOLOGY

Illustrated by LESLIE C BENENSON RE

This Anthology first published in 1990 by Padda Books, Bexhill-on-Sea, East Sussex

ISBN 0 9515786 0 X

Design and Production by John Saunders, Practical Design, Reading
Printed and bound in Great Britain by
MacLehose & Partners, Portsmouth

Padda Books

And he told the Ox of a manger
And a stall in Bethlehem,
And he spoke to the Ass of a Rider
That rode to Jerusalem.

They steamed and dripped in the chancel
They listened and never stirred
While, just as though they were Bishops,
Eddi preached them the word.

Till the gale blew off the marshes
And the windows showed the day
And the Ox and the Ass together
Wheeled and clattered away.

And when the Saxons mocked him
Said Eddi of Manhood End,
'I dare not shut His chapel
On such as care to attend.'

Rudyard Kipling *This poem introduced the story 'The Conversion of St. Wilfrid' from 'Rewards and Fairies'*

Eddi's Service

Eddi, priest of St. Wilfrid
In the chapel at Manhood End,
Ordered a midnight service
For such as cared to attend.

But the Saxons were keeping Christmas,
And the night was stormy as well.
Nobody came to the service,
Though Eddi rang the bell.

'Wicked weather for walking.'
Said Eddi of Manhood End
'But I must go on with the service
For such as care to attend.'

The altar candles were lighted,–
An old marsh-donkey came,
Bold as a guest invited,
And stared at the guttering flame.

The storm beat on at the windows,
The water splashed on the floor,
And a wet, yoke-weary bullock
Pushed in through the open door.

'How do I know what is greatest,
How do I know what is least?
That is my Father's business,'
Said Eddi, Wilfrid's priest.

'But–three are gathered together–
Listen to me and attend.
I bring good news, my brethren!'
Said Eddi of Manhood End.

For R K

Compiled by Rosemary Mitchell and Joan M Vann

Batemans
15 June 1989

Foreword

For whoever pays the taxes Old Mus' Hobden owns the Land.

RUDYARD KIPLING'S love of Sussex goes back to a time long before he went to live at Batemans in Burwash. He left the United Services College at the end of the Summer term in 1882, and stayed in Rottingdean with the beloved Aunt and Uncle (the Burne-Jones') until he sailed for India and his 'Seven years hard'.

You might say that he had mild love affairs with many places – Lahore, Simla, Mandalay, and then Vermont – until the shadows of a family quarrel and the death of his daughter Josephine came between them, and again, Rottingdean, until his fame and popularity made living in The Elms impossible.

But in 1902 he came to live in the 'Very Own House', a place where he could 'raise his kids, build a wall, dig a well and plant a tree' and in his verse and his prose he told the world that this was where he would put down his roots. It would not be easy to call to mind all the ways in which Kipling tells us that this, finally, was the home that he had been seeking, but it is hoped that this anthology will remind you of some of them.

In a letter to C.E. Norton in November 1902 he wrote 'Then we discovered England which we had never done before, and went to live in it. . . It is made up of trees and green fields and mud and the gentry, and at last I'm one of the gentry.' It is not certain that he was really one of the gentry. Perhaps because he avoided any involvement in local affairs, and because many of his friends came from overseas, he was never really accepted as 'gentry', but he made up for this by getting to know the Hobdens and the Isteds, and by picturing them with his unfailing pen.

In every one of the stories and verses in this book you will find yourself sharing with Kipling a deep and lasting love of the land, and an understanding of its people – their hopes and fears, their traditions, their thoughts and their speech – and becoming in truth, a part of our own lovely county of Sussex.

RONALD KING

A Three-part Song

I'M JUST in love with all these three,
The Weald and the Marsh and the Down countree.
Nor I don't know which I love the most,
The Weald or the Marsh or the white Chalk coast!

I've buried my heart in a ferny hill,
Twix' a liddle low shaw an' a great high gill.
Oh, hop-bine yaller an' wood-smoke blue,
I reckon you'll keep her middling true!

I've loosed my mind for to out and run
On a Marsh that was old when Kings begun.
Oh, Romney Level and Brenzett reeds,
I reckon you know what my mind needs!

I've given my soul to the Southdown grass,
And sheep-bells tinkled where you pass.
Oh, Firle an' Ditchling an' sails at sea,
I reckon you keep my soul for me!

PUCK OF POOK'S HILL

Puck's Song

SEE you the ferny ride that steals
Into the oak-woods far?
O that was whence they hewed the keels
That rolled to Trafalgar.

And mark you where the ivy clings
To Bayham's mouldering walls?
O there we cast the stout railings
That stand around St. Paul's.

See you the dimpled track that runs
All hollow through the wheat?
O that was where they hauled the guns
That smote King Philip's fleet.

(Out of the Weald, the secret Weald,
Men sent in ancient years
The horse-shoes red at Flodden Field,
The arrows at Poitiers!)

See you our little mill that clacks,
So busy by the brook?
She has ground her corn and paid her tax
Ever since Domesday Book.

See you our stilly woods of oak,
And the dread ditch beside?
O that was where the Saxons broke
On the day that Harold died.

See you the windy levels spread
About the gates of Rye?
O that was where the Northmen fled,
When Alfred's ships came by.

See you our pastures wide and lone,
Where the red oxen browse?
O there was a City thronged and known,
Ere London boasted a house.

And see you, after rain, the trace
Of mound and ditch and wall?
O that was a Legion's camping-place,
When Cæsar sailed from Gaul.

And see you marks that show and fade,
Like shadows on the Downs?
O they are the lines the Flint Men made,
To guard their wondrous towns.

Trackway and Camp and City lost,
Salt Marsh where now is corn –
Old Wars, old Peace, old Arts that cease,
And so was England born!

She is not any common Earth,
Water or wood or air,
But Merlin's Isle of Gramarye,
Where you and I will fare!

PUCK OF POOK'S HILL

THEN they walked through the grass to the knoll where Little Lindens stands. The old farmhouse, weather-tiled to the ground, took almost the colour of a blood-ruby in the afternoon light. The pigeons pecked at the mortar in the chimney-stacks; the bees that had lived under the tiles since it was built filled the hot August air with their booming; and the smell of the box-tree by the dairy-window mixed with the smell of earth after rain, bread after baking, and a tickle of wood-smoke.

The farmer's wife came to the door, baby on arm, shaded her brows against the sun, stooped to pluck a sprig of rosemary, and turned down the orchard. The old spaniel in his barrel barked once or twice to show he was in charge of the empty house. Puck clicked back the garden-gate.

'D'you marvel that I love it?' said Hal, in a whisper. 'What can town folk know of the nature of housen – or land?'

They perched themselves arow on the old hacked oak bench in Lindens garden, looking across the valley of the

brook at the fern-covered dimples and hollows of the Forge behind Hobden's cottage. The old man was cutting a faggot in his garden by the hives. It was quite a second after his chopper fell that the chump of the blow reached their lazy ears.

'Eh – yeh!' said Hal. 'I mind when where that old gaffer stands was Nether Forge – Master John Collins's foundry. Many a night has his big trip-hammer shook me in my bed here. *Boom-bitty! Boom-bitty!* If the wind was east, I could hear Master Tom Collins's forge at Stockens answering his brother, *Boom-opp! Boom-oop!* and midway between, Sir John Pelham's sledge-hammers at Brightling would strike in like a pack o' scholars, and "*Hic-haec-hoc*" they'd say, "*Hic-haec-hoc*," till I fell asleep. Yes. The valley was as full o' forges and fineries as a May shaw o' cuckoos. All gone to grass now!'

'What did they make?' said Dan.

'Guns for the King's ships – and for others. Serpentines and cannon mostly. When the guns were cast, down would come the King's Officers, and take our plough-oxen to haul them to the coast.

HAL O' THE DRAFT

JUST beyond the west fringe of our land, in a little valley running from Nowhere to Nothing-at-all, stood the long, over-grown slag-heap of a most ancient forge, supposed to have been worked by the Phoenicians and Romans and, since then, uninterruptedly till the middle of the eighteenth century. The bracken and rush-patches still hid stray pigs of iron, and if one scratched a few inches through the rabbit-shaven turf, one came on the narrow mule-tracks of peacock-hued furnace-slag laid down in Elizabeth's day. The ghost of a road climbed up out of this dead arena, and crossed our fields, where it was known as 'The Gunway,' and popularly connected with Armada times. Every foot of that little corner was alive with ghosts and shadows.

SOMETHING OF MYSELF

The Way Through The Woods

THEY shut the road through the woods
Seventy years ago.
Weather and rain have undone it again,
And now you would never know
There was once a road through the woods
Before they planted the trees.
It is underneath the coppice and heath
And the thin anemones.
Only the keeper sees
That, where the ring-dove broods,
And the badgers roll at ease,
There was once a road through the woods.

Yet, if you enter the woods
Of a summer evening late,
When the night-air cools on the trout-ringed pools
Where the otter whistles his mate,
(They fear not men in the woods,
Because they see so few.)
You will hear the beat of a horse's feet,
And the swish of a skirt in the dew,
Steadily cantering through
The misty solitudes,
As though they perfectly knew
The old lost road through the woods. . .
But there is no road through the woods.

REWARDS AND FAIRIES

Alnaschar and The Oxen

THERE'S a pasture in a valley where the hanging woods divide,
And a Herd lies down and ruminates in peace;
Where the pheasant rules the nooning, and the owl the twilight-tide,
And the war-cries of our world die out and cease.
Here I cast aside the burden that each weary week-day brings
And, delivered from the shadows I pursue,
On peaceful, postless Sabbaths I consider Weighty Things –
Such as Sussex Cattle feeding in the dew!

At the gate beside the river where the trouty shallows brawl,
I know the pride that Lobengula felt,
When he bade the bars be lowered of the Royal Cattle Kraal,
And fifteen miles of oxen took the veldt.
From the walls of Bulawayo in unbroken file they came
To where the Mount of Council cuts the blue . . .
I have only six and twenty, but the principle's the same
With my Sussex Cattle feeding in the dew!

To a luscious sound of tearing, where the clovered herbage rips,
Level-backed and level-bellied watch 'em move –
See those shoulders, guess that heart-girth, praise those loins, admire those hips,
And the tail set low for flesh to make above!
Count the broad unblemished muzzles, test the kindly mellow skin,
And, where yon heifer lifts her head at call,
Mark the bosom's just abundance 'neath the gay and clean-cut chin,
And those eyes of Juno, overlooking all!

Here is colour, form and substance! I will put it to the proof
  And, next season, in my lodges shall be born
Some very Bull of Mithras, flawless from his agate hoof
  To his even-branching, ivory, dusk-tipped horn.
He shall mate with block-square virgins – kings shall seek his like in vain,
  While I multiply his stock a thousandfold,
Till an hungry world extol me, builder of a lofty strain
  That turns one standard ton at two years old!

There's a valley, under oakwood, where a man may dream his dream,
  In the milky breath of cattle laid at ease,
Till the moon o'ertops the alders, and her image chills the stream,
  And the river-mist runs silver round their knees!
Now the footpaths fade and vanish; now the ferny clumps deceive;
  Now the hedgerow-folk possess their fields anew;
Now the Herd is lost in darkness, and I bless them as I leave,
  My Sussex Cattle feeding in the dew!

DEBITS AND CREDITS

'HAVE you ever bin in the Marsh?' he said to Dan.

'Only as far as Rye, once,' Dan answered.

'Ah, that's but the edge. Back behind of her there's steeples settin' beside churches, an' wise women settin' beside their doors, an' the sea settin' above the land, an' ducks herdin' wild in the diks' (he meant ditches). 'The Marsh is justabout riddled with diks an' sluices, an' tide-gates an' water-lets. You can hear 'em bubblin' an' grummelin' when the tide works in 'em, an' then you hear the sea rangin' left and right-handed all up along the Wall. You've seen how flat she is – the Marsh? You'd think nothin' easier than to walk eend-on acrost her? Ah, but the diks an' the water-lets, they twists the roads about as ravelly as witch-yarn on the spindles. So ye get all turned round in broad daylight.'

'That's because they've dreened the waters into the diks,' said Hobden. 'When I courted my woman the rushes was green – Eh me! the rushes was green – an' the Bailiff o' the Marshes, he rode up and down as free as the fog.'

'Who was he?' said Dan.

'Why, the Marsh fever an' ague. He's clapped me on the shoulder once or twice till I shook proper. But now the dreenin' off of the waters have done away with the fevers; so they make a joke, like, that the Bailiff o' the Marshes broke his neck in a dik. A won'erful place for bees an' ducks 'tis too.'

DYMCHURCH FLIT

A Smuggler's Song

IF YOU wake at midnight, and hear a horse's feet,
Don't go drawing back the blind, or looking in the street,
Them that asks no questions isn't told a lie.
Watch the wall, my darling, while the Gentlemen go by!
        Five and twenty ponies
        Trotting through the dark –
        Brandy for the Parson,
        'Baccy for the Clerk;
        Laces for a lady, letters for a spy,
And watch the wall, my darling, while the Gentlemen go by!

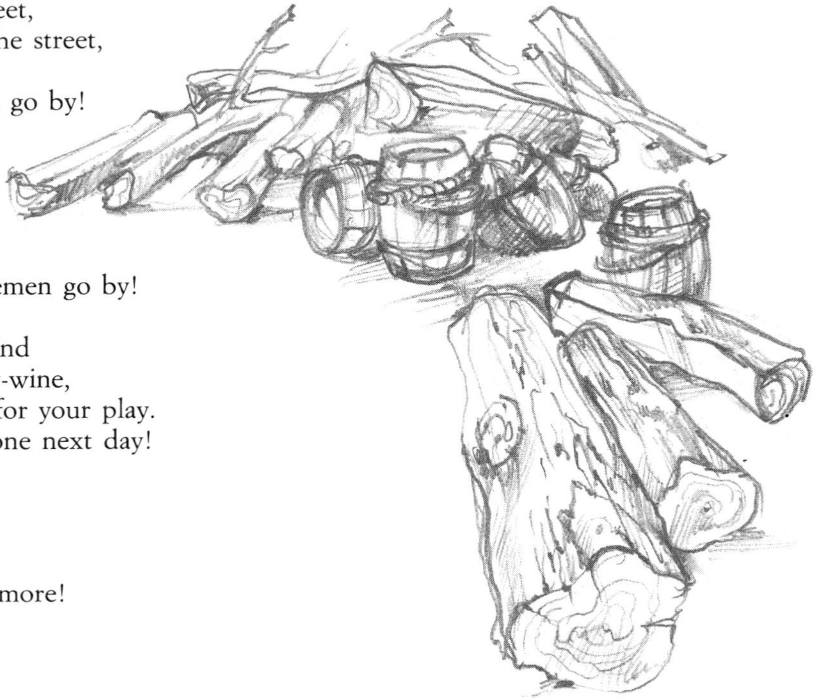

Running round the woodlump if you chance to find
Little barrels, roped and tarred, all full of brandy-wine,
Don't you shout to come and look, nor use 'em for your play.
Put the brishwood back again – and they'll be gone next day!

If you see the stable-door setting open wide;
If you see a tired horse lying down inside;
If your mother mends a coat cut about and tore;
If the lining's wet and warm – don't you ask no more!

If you meet King George's men, dressed in blue and red,
You be careful what you say, and mindful what is said.
If they call you 'pretty maid,' and chuck you 'neath the chin,
Don't you tell where no one is, nor yet where no one's been!

Knocks and footsteps round the house – whistles after dark –
You've no call for running out till the house-dogs bark.
Trusty's here, and *Pincher's* here, and see how dumb they lie –
They don't fret to follow when the Gentlemen go by!

If you do as you've been told, 'likely there's a chance,
You'll be give a dainty doll, all the way from France,
With a cap of Valenciennes, and a velvet hood –
A present from the Gentlemen, along o' being good!
        Five and twenty ponies
        Trotting through the dark –
        Brandy for the Parson,
        'Baccy for the Clerk.
Them that asks no questions isn't told a lie –
Watch the wall, my darling, while the Gentlemen go by!

PUCK OF POOK'S HILL

The Flight

WHEN the grey geese heard the Fool's tread
   Too near to where they lay,
They lifted neither voice nor head,
   But took themselves away.

No water broke, no pinion whirred –
   There went no warning call.
The steely, sheltering rushes stirred
   A little – that was all.

Only the osiers understood,
   And the drowned meadows spied
What else than wreckage of a flood
   Stole outward on that tide.

But the far beaches saw their ranks
   Gather and greet and grow
By myriads on the naked banks
   Watching their sign to go;

Till, with a roar of wings that churned
   The shivering shoals to foam,
Flight after flight took air and turned
   To find a safer home;

And, far below their steadfast wedge,
   They heard (and hastened on)
Men thresh and clamour through the sedge
   Aghast that they were gone!

And, when men prayed them come anew
   And nest where they were bred,
'Nay, fools foretell what knaves will do,'
   Was all the grey geese said.

COLLECTED VERSE

Eddi's Service

(A. D. 687)

EDDI, priest of St. Wilfrid
   In his chapel at Manhood End,
Ordered a midnight service
   For such as cared to attend.

But the Saxons were keeping Christmas,
   And the night was stormy as well.
Nobody came to service,
   Though Eddi rang the bell.

'Wicked weather for walking.'
   Said Eddi of Manhood End.
'But I must go on with the service
   For such as care to attend.'

The altar-lamps were lighted, –
   An old marsh-donkey came,
Bold as a guest invited,
   And stared at the guttering flame.

The storm beat on at the windows,
   The water splashed on the floor,
And a wet, yoke-weary bullock
   Pushed in through the open door.

'How do I know what is greatest,
   How do I know what is least?
That is My Father's business,'
   Said Eddi, Wilfrid's priest.

'But – three are gathered together –
   Listen to me and attend.
I bring good news, my brethren!'
   Said Eddi of Manhood End.

And he told the Ox of a Manger
   And a Stall in Bethlehem,
And he spoke to the Ass of a Rider
   That rode to Jerusalem.

They steamed and dripped in the chancel,
   They listened and never stirred,
While, just as though they were Bishops,
   Eddi preached them The Word,

Till the gale blew off on the marshes
   And the windows showed the day,
And the Ox and the Ass together
   Wheeled and clattered away.

And when the Saxons mocked him,
   Said Eddi of Manhood End,
'I dare not shut His chapel
   On such as care to attend.'

REWARDS AND FAIRIES

THE new Church Visitor had just left after a twenty minutes' call. During that time, Mrs. Ashcroft had used such English as an elderly, experienced, and pensioned cook should, who had seen life in London. She was the readier, therefore, to slip back into easy, ancient Sussex ('t's softening to 'd's as one warmed) when the 'bus brought Mrs. Fettley from thirty miles away for a visit, that pleasant March Saturday. The two had been friends since childhood; but, of late, destiny had separated their meetings by long intervals.

Much was to be said, and many ends, loose since last time, to be ravelled up on both sides, before Mrs. Fettley, with her bag of quilt-patches, took the couch beneath the window commanding the garden, and the football-ground in the valley below.

'Most folk got out at Bush Tye for the match there,' she explained, 'so there weren't no one for me to cushion agin, the last five mile. An' she *do* just-about bounce ye.'

'You've took no hurt,' said her hostess. 'You don't brittle by agein', Liz.'

Mrs. Fettley chuckled and made to match a couple of patches to her liking. 'No, or I'd ha' broke twenty year back. You can't ever mind when I was so's to be called round, can ye?'

Mrs. Ashcroft shook her head slowly – she never hurried – and went on stitching a sack-cloth lining into a list-bound rush tool-basket. Mrs. Fettley laid out more patches in the Spring light through the geraniums on the window-sill, and they were silent awhile.

'What like's this new Visitor o' yourn?' Mrs. Fettley inquired, with a nod towards the door. Being very short-sighted, she had, on her entrance, almost bumped into the lady.

Mrs. Ashcroft suspended the big packing-needle judicially on high, ere she stabbed home. 'Settin' aside she don't bring much news with her yet, I dunno as I've anythin' special agin her.'

'Ourn, at Keyneslade,' said Mrs. Fettley, 'she's full o' words an' pity, but she don't stay for answers. Ye can get on with your thoughts while she clacks.'

'This 'un don't clack. She's aimin' to be one o' those High Church nuns, like.'

'Ourn's married, but, by what they say, she've made no great gains of it . . .' Mrs. Fettley threw up her sharp chin. 'Lord! How they dam' cherubim do shake the very bones o' the place!'

The tile-sided cottage trembled at the passage of two specially chartered forty-seat charabancs on their way to the Bush Tye match; a regular Saturday 'shopping' 'bus, for the county's capital, fumed behind them; while, from one of the crowded inns, a fourth car backed out to join the procession, and held up the stream of through pleasure-traffic.

'You're as free-tongued as ever, Liz,' Mrs. Ashcroft observed.

THE WISH HOUSE

Sussex

GOD gave all men all earth to love,
But, since our hearts are small,
Ordained for each one spot should prove
  Beloved over all;
That, as He watched Creation's birth,
  So we, in godlike mood,
May of our love create our earth
  And see that it is good.

So one shall Baltic pines content,
  As one some Surrey glade,
Or one the palm-grove's droned lament
  Before Levuka's Trade.
Each to his choice, and I rejoice
  The lot has fallen to me
In a fair ground – in a fair ground –
  Yea, Sussex by the sea!

No tender-hearted garden crowns,
  No bosomed woods adorn
Our blunt, bow-headed, whale-backed Downs,
  But gnarled and writhen thorn –
Bare slopes where chasing shadows skim,
  And, through the gaps revealed,
Belt upon belt, the wooded, dim,
  Blue goodness of the Weald.

Clean of officious fence or hedge,
  Half-wild and wholly tame,
The wise turf cloaks the white cliff-edge
  As when the Romans came.
What sign of those that fought and died
  At shift of sword and sword?
The barrow and the camp abide,
  The sunlight and the sward.

Here leaps ashore the full Sou'west
  All heavy-winged with brine,
Here lies above the folded crest
  The Channel's leaden line;
And here the sea-fogs lap and cling,
  And here, each warning each,
The sheep-bells and the ship-bells ring
  Along the hidden beach.

We have no waters to delight
  Our broad and brookless vales –
Only the dewpond on the height
  Unfed, that never fails –
Whereby no tattered herbage tells
  Which way the season flies –
Only our close-bit thyme that smells
  Like dawn in Paradise.

Here through the strong and shadeless days
  The tinkling silence thrills;
Or little, lost, Down churches praise
  The Lord who made the hills:
But here the Old Gods guard their round,
  And, in her secret heart
The heathen kingdom Wilfrid found
  Dreams, as she dwells, apart.

Though all the rest were all my share,
  With equal soul I'd see
Her nine-and-thirty sister fair,
  Yet none more fair than she.
Choose ye your need from Thames to Tweed,
  And I will choose instead
Such lands as lie 'twixt Rake and Rye,
  Black Down and Beachy Head.

I will go out against the sun
  Where the rolled scarp retires,
And the Long Man of Wilmington
  Looks naked toward the shires;
And east till doubling Rother crawls
  To find the fickle tide,
By dry and sea-forgotten walls,
  Our ports of stranded pride.

I will go north about the shaws
   And the deep ghylls that breed
Huge oaks and old, the which we hold
   No more than Sussex weed;
Or south where windy Piddinghoe's
   Begilded dolphine veers,
   And red beside wide-bankèd Ouse
      Lie down our Sussex steers.

So to the land our hearts we give
   Till the sure magic strike,
And Memory, Use, and Love make live
   Us and our field alike –
That deeper than our speech and thought,
   Beyond our reason's sway,
Clay of the pit whence we were wrought
   Yearns to its fellow-clay.

God gives all men all earth to love,
   But, since man's heart is small,
Ordains for each one spot shall prove
   Belovèd over all.
Each to his choice, and I rejoice
   The lot has fallen to me
In a fair ground – in a fair ground –
   Yea, Sussex by the sea!

COLLECTED VERSE

The Run of The Downs

THE Weald is good, the Downs are best –
I'll give you the run of 'em, East to West.
Beachy Head and Winddoor Hill,
They were once and they are still.
Firle, Mount Caburn and Mount Harry
Go back as far as sums'll carry.
Ditchling Beacon and Chanctonbury Ring,
They have looked on many a thing,
And what those two have missed between 'em,
I reckon Truleigh Hill has seen 'em.
Highden, Bignor and Duncton Down
Knew Old England before the Crown.
Linch Down, Treyford and Sunwood
Knew Old England before the Flood;
And when you end on the Hampshire side –
Butser's old as Time and Tide.
The Downs are sheep, the Weald is corn,
You be glad you are Sussex born!

REWARDS AND FAIRIES

ONE view called me to another; one hill top to its fellow, half across the county, and since I could answer at no more trouble than the snapping forward of a lever, I let the county flow under my wheels. The orchid-studded flats of the East gave way to the thyme, ilex, and grey grass of the Downs; these again to the rich cornland and fig-trees of the lower coast, where you carry the beat of the tide on your left hand for fifteen level miles; and when at last I turned inland through a huddle of rounded hills and woods I had run myself clean out of my known marks.

Beyond that precise hamlet which stands godmother to the capital of the United States, I found hidden villages where bees, the only things awake, boomed in eighty-foot lindens that overhung grey Norman churches; miraculous brooks diving under stone bridges built for heavier traffic than would ever vex them again; tithe-barns larger than their churches, and an old smithy that cried out aloud how it had once been a hall of the Knights of the Temple. Gipsies I found on a common where the gorse, bracken, and heath fought it out together up a mile of Roman road; and a little farther on I disturbed a red fox rolling dog-fashion in the naked sunlight.

THEY

THERE came at last a brilliant day, swept clear from the south-west, that brought the hills within hand's reach – a day of unstable airs and high filmy clouds. Through no merit of my own I was free, and set the car for the third time on that known road. As I reached the crest of the Downs I felt the soft air change, saw it glaze under the sun; and, looking down at the sea, in that instant beheld the blue of the Channel turn through polished silver and dulled steel to dingy pewter. A laden collier hugging the coast steered outward for deeper water, and, across copper-coloured haze, I saw sails rise one by one on the anchored fishing-fleet. In a deep dene behind me an eddy of sudden wind drummed through sheltered oaks, and spun aloft the first dry sample of autumn leaves. When I reached the beach road the sea-fog fumed over the brickfields, and the tide was telling all the groins of the gale beyond Ushant. In less than an hour summer England vanished in chill grey. We were again the shut island of the North, all the ships of the world bellowing at our perilous gates; and between their outcries ran the piping of bewildered gulls. My cap dripped moisture, the folds of the rug held it in pools or sluiced it away in runnels, and the salt-rime stuck to my lips.

THEY

A Charm

TAKE of English earth as much
As either hand may rightly clutch.
In the taking of it breathe
Prayer for all who lie beneath.
Not the great nor well-bespoke,
But the mere uncounted folk
Of whose life and death is none
Report or lamentation.
   Lay that earth upon thy heart,
   And thy sickness shall depart!

It shall sweeten and make whole
Fevered breath and festered soul.
It shall mightily restrain
Over-busied hand and brain.
It shall ease thy mortal strife
'Gainst the immortal woe of life,
Till thyself, restored, shall prove
By what grace the Heavens do move

Take of English flowers these –
Spring's full-facèd primroses,
Summer's wild wide-hearted rose,
Autumn's wall-flower of the close,
And, thy darkness to illume,
Winter's bee-thronged ivy-bloom.
Seek and serve them where they bide
From Candlemas to Christmas-tide,
   For these simples, used aright,
   Can restore a failing sight.

These shall cleanse and purify
Webbed and inward-turning eye;
These shall show thee treasure hid
Thy familiar fields amid;
And reveal (which is thy need)
Every man a King indeed!

REWARDS AND FAIRIES

Cuckoo Song

(Spring begins in Southern England on the 14th April, on which date the Old Woman lets the Cuckoo out of her basket at Heathfield Fair – locally known as Heffle Cuckoo Fair.)

TELL it to the locked-up trees,
Cuckoo, bring your song here!
Warrant, Act and Summons, please,
For Spring to pass along here!
Tell old Winter, if he doubt,
Tell him squat and square – a!
Old Woman!
Old Woman!
Old Woman's let the Cuckoo out
At Heffle Cuckoo Fair – a!

March has searched and April tried –
'Tisn't long to May now.
Not so far to Whitsuntide
And Cuckoo's come to stay now!
Hear the valiant fellow shout
Down the orchard bare – a!
Old Woman!
Old Woman!
Old Woman's let the Cuckoo out
At Heffle Cuckoo Fair – a!

When your heart is young and gay
And the season rules it –
Work your works and play your play
'Fore the Autumn cools it!
Kiss you turn and turn-about,
But, my lad, beware – a!
Old Woman!
Old Woman!
Old Woman's let the Cuckoo out
At Heffle Cuckoo Fair – a!

COLLECTED VERSE

THE children went to the seaside for a month, and lived in a flint village on the bare windy chalk Downs, quite thirty miles away from home. They made friends with an old shepherd, called Mr. Dudeney, who had known their Father when their Father was little. He did not talk like their own people in the Weald of Sussex, and he used different names for farm things, but he understood how they felt, and let them go with him. He had a tiny cottage about half a mile from the village, where his wife made mead from thyme honey, and nursed sick lambs in front of a coal fire, while Old Jim, who was Mr. Dudeney's sheep-dog's father, lay at the door. They brought up beef bones for Old Jim (you must never give a sheep-dog mutton bones), and if Mr. Dudeney happened to be far in the Downs, Mrs. Dudeney would tell the dog to take them to him, and he did.

One August afternoon when the village water-cart had made the street smell specially townified, they went to look for their shepherd as usual, and, as usual, Old Jim crawled over the door-step and took them in charge. The sun was hot, the dry grass was very slippery, and the distances were very distant.

'It's just like the sea,' said Una, when Old Jim halted in the shade of a lonely flint barn on a bare rise. 'You see where you're going, and – you go there, and there's nothing between.'

Dan slipped off his shoes. 'When we get home I shall sit in the woods all day,' he said.

'Whuff!' said Old Jim, to show he was ready, and struck across a long rolling stretch of turf. Presently he asked for his beef bone.

'Not yet,' said Dan. 'Where's Mr. Dudeney? Where's Master?'

Old Jim looked as if he thought they were mad, and asked again.

'Don't you give it him,' Una cried. 'I'm not going to be left howling in a desert.'

'Show, boy! Show!' said Dan, for the Downs seemed as bare as the palm of your hand.

Old Jim sighed, and trotted forward. Soon they spied the blob of Mr. Dudeney's hat against the sky a long way off.

'Right! All right!' said Dan. Old Jim wheeled round, took his bone carefully between his blunted teeth, and returned to the shadow of the old barn, looking just like a wolf. The children went on. Two kestrels hung bivvering and squealing above them. A gull flapped lazily along the white edge of the cliffs. The curves of the Downs shook a little in the heat, and so did Mr. Dudeney's distant head.

They walked toward it very slowly and found themselves staring into a horseshoe-shaped hollow a hundred feet deep, whose steep sides were laced with tangled sheep-tracks. The flock grazed on the flat at the bottom, under charge of Young Jim. Mr. Dudeney sat comfortably knitting on the edge of the slope, his crook between his kness. They told him what Old Jim had done.

'Ah, he thought you could see my head as soon as he did. The closeter you be to the turf the more you see things. You look warm-like,' said Mr. Dudeney.

'We be,' said Una, flopping down. '*And* tired.'

'Set beside o' me here. The shadow'll begin to stretch out in a little while, and a heat-shake o' wind will come up with it that'll overlay your eyes like so much wool.'

'We don't want to sleep,' said Una indignantly; but she settled herself as she spoke, in the first strip of early afternoon shade.

'O' course not. You come to talk with me same as your father used. *He* didn't need no dog to guide him to Norton Pit.'

'Well, he belonged here,' said Dan, and laid himself down at length on the turf.

'He did. And what beats me is why he went off to live among them messy trees in the Weald, when he might ha' stayed here and looked all about him. There's no profit to trees. They draw the lightning, and sheep shelter under 'em, and *so*, like as not, you'll lose a half-score ewes struck dead in one storm. Tck! Your father knew that.'

'Trees aren't messy.' Una rose on her elbow. 'And what about firewood? I don't like coal.'

'Eh? You lie a piece more uphill and you'll lie more natural,' said Mr Dudeney, with his provoking deaf smile. 'Now press your face down and smell to the turf. That's Southdown thyme which makes our Southdown mutton beyond compare, and, my mother told me, 'twill cure anything except broken necks, or hearts. I forget which.'

They sniffed, and somehow forgot to lift their cheeks from the soft thymy cushions.

'You don't get nothing like that in the Weald. Watercress, maybe?' said Mr. Dudeney.

'But we've water – brooks full of it – where you paddle in hot weather,' Una replied, watching a yellow-and-violet-banded snail-shell close to her eye.

'Brooks flood. Then you must shift your sheep – let alone foot-rot afterward. I put more dependence on a dew-pond any day.'

'How's a dew-pond made?' said Dan, and tilted his hat over his eyes. Mr. Dudeney explained.

The air trembled a little as though it could not make up its mind whether to slide into the Pit or move across the open. But it seemed easiest to go downhill, and the children felt one soft puff after another slip and sidle down the slope in fragrant breaths that baffed on their eyelids. The little whisper of the sea by the cliffs joined with the whisper of the wind over the grass, the hum of insects in the thyme, the ruffle and rustle of the flock below, and a thickish mutter deep in the very chalk beneath them. Mr. Dudeney stopped explaining, and went on with his knitting.

THE KNIFE AND THE NAKED CHALK

A Tree Song

OF ALL the trees that grow so fair,
Old England to adorn,
Greater are none beneath the Sun
  Than Oak, and Ash, and Thorn.
Sing Oak, and Ash, and Thorn, good sirs,
  (All of a Midsummer morn!)
Surely we sing no little thing
  In Oak, and Ash, and Thorn!

Oak of Clay lived many a day
  Or ever Æneas began.
Ash of the Loam was a lady at home
  When Brut was an outlaw man.
Thorn of the Down saw New Troy Town
  (From which was London born);
Witness hereby the ancientry
  Of Oak, and Ash, and Thorn!

Yew that is old in churchyard-mould,
  He breedeth a mighty bow.
Alder for shoes do wise men choose,
  And beech for cups also.
But when ye have killed, and your bowl is spilled,
  And your shoes are clean outworn,
Back ye must speed for all that ye need
  To Oak, and Ash, and Thorn!

Ellum she hateth mankind, and waiteth
  Till every gust be laid
To drop a limb on the head of him
  That anyway trusts her shade.
But whether a lad be sober or sad,
  Or mellow with ale from the horn,
He will take no wrong when he lieth along
  'Neath Oak, and Ash, and Thorn!

Oh, do not tell the Priest our plight,
  Or he would call it a sin;
But – we have been out in the woods all night,
  A-conjuring Summer in!
And we bring you news by word of mouth –
  Good news for cattle and corn –
Now is the Sun come up from the South
  With Oak, and Ash, and Thorn!

Sing Oak, and Ash, and Thorn, good sirs
  (All of a Midsummer morn)!
England shall bide till Judgment Tide
  By Oak, and Ash, and Thorn!

PUCK OF POOK'S HILL

Norman and Saxon

(A. D. 1100)

'MY SON,' said the Norman Baron, 'I am dying, and you will be heir
To all the broad acres in England that William gave me for my share
When we conquered the Saxon at Hastings, and a nice little handful it is.
But before you go over to rule it I want you to understand this:–

'The Saxon is not like us Normans. His manners are not so polite.
But he never means anything serious till he talks about justice and right.
When he stands like an ox in the furrow with his sullen set eyes on your own,
And grumbles, 'This isn't fair dealing,' my son, leave the Saxon alone.

'You can horsewhip your Gascony archers, or torture your Picardy spears;
But don't try that game on the Saxon; you'll have the whole brood round your ears.
From the richest old Thane in the county to the poorest chained serf in the field,
They'll be at you and on you like hornets, and, if you are wise, you will yield.

'But first you must master their language, their dialect,
  proverbs and songs.
Don't trust any clerk to interpret when they come with
  the tale of their wrongs.
Let them know that you know what they're saying; let
  them feel that you know what to say.
Yes, even when you want to go hunting, hear 'em out if it
  takes you all day.

'They'll drink every hour of the daylight and poach every
  hour of the dark.
It's the sport not the rabbits they're after (we've plenty of
  game in the park).
Don't hang them or cut off their fingers. That's wasteful
  as well as unkind.
For a hard-bitten, South-country poacher makes the best
  man-at-arms you can find.

'Appear with your wife and the children at their
  weddings and funerals and feasts.
Be polite but not friendly to Bishops; be good to all poor
  parish priests.
Say "we," "us" and "ours" when you're talking, instead
  of "you fellows" and "I."
Don't ride over seeds; keep your temper; and *never you
  tell 'em a lie!*'

COLLECTED VERSE

THE valley was so choked with fog that one could scarcely see a cow's length across a field. Every blade, twig, bracken-frond, and hoof-print carried water, and the air was filled with the noise of rushing ditches and field-drains, all delivering to the brook below. A week's November rain on water-logged land had gorged her to full flood, and she proclaimed it aloud.

Two men in sackcloth aprons were considering an untrimmed hedge that ran down the hillside and disappeared into mist beside those roarings. They stood back and took stock of the neglected growth, tapped an elbow of hedge-oak here, a mossed beech-stub there, swayed a stooled ash back and forth, and looked at each other.

'I reckon she's about two rod thick,' said Jabez the younger, 'an' she hasn't felt iron since – when has she, Jesse?'

'Call it twenty-five year, Jabez, an' you won't be far out.'

'Umm!' Jabez rubbed his wet handbill on his wetter coat-sleeve. 'She ain't a hedge. She's all manner o' trees. We'll just about have to—' He paused, as professional etiquette required.

'Just about have to side her up an' see what she'll bear. But hadn't we best—?' Jesse paused in his turn, both men being artists and equals.

'Get some kind o' line to go by.' Jabez ranged up and down till he found a thinner place, and with clean snicks of the handbill revealed the original face of the fence. Jesse took over the dripping stuff as it fell forward, and, with a grasp and a kick, made it to lie orderly on the bank till it should be faggoted.

By noon a length of unclean jungle had turned itself into a cattle-proof barrier, tufted here and there with little plumes of the sacred holly which no woodman touches without orders.

'Now we've a witness-board to go by!' said Jesse at last.

'She won't be as easy as this all along,' Jabez answered. 'She'll need plenty stakes and binders when we come to the brook.'

'Well, ain't we plenty?' Jesse pointed to the ragged

perspective ahead of them that plunged downhill into the fog. 'I lay there's a cord an' a half o' firewood, let alone faggots, 'fore we get anywheres anigh the brook.'

'The brook's got up a piece since morning,' said Jabez. 'Sounds like's if she was over Wickenden's door-stones.'

Jesse listened, too. There was a growl in the brook's roar as though she worried something hard.

'Yes. She's over Wickenden's door-stones,' he replied. 'Now she'll flood acrost Alder Bay an' that'll ease her.'

'She won't ease Jim Wickenden's hay none if she do,' Jabez grunted. 'I told Jim he'd set that liddle hay-stack o' his too low down in the medder. I *told* him so when he was drawin' the bottom for it.'

'I told him so, too,' said Jesse. 'I told him 'fore ever you did. I told him when the County Council tarred the roads up along.' He pointed up-hill, where unseen automobiles and road-engines droned past continually. 'A tarred road, she shoots every drop o' water into a valley same's a slate roof. 'Tisn't as 'twas in the old days, when the waters soaked in and soaked out in the way o' nature. It rooshes off they tarred roads all of a lump, and naturally every drop is bound to descend into the valley. And there's tar roads both two sides this valley for ten mile. That's what I told Jim Wickenden when they tarred the roads last year. But he's a valley-man. He don't hardly ever journey up-hill.'

FRIENDLY BROOK

The Land

WHEN Julius Fabricius, Sub-Prefect of the Weald,
In the days of Diocletian owned our Lower River-field,
He called to him Hobdenius – a Briton of the Clay,
Saying: 'What about that River-piece for layin' in to hay?'

And the aged Hobden answered: 'I remember as a lad
My father told your father that she wanted dreenin' bad.
An' the more that you neglect her the less you'll get her
  clean.
Have it jest *as* you've a mind to, but, if I was you, I'd
  dreen.'

So they drained it long and crossways in the lavish
  Roman style –
Still we find among the river-drift their flakes of ancient
  tile,
And in drouthy middle August, when the bones of
  meadows show,
We can trace the lines they followed sixteen hundred
  years ago.

Then Julius Fabricius died as even Prefects do,
And after certain centuries, Imperial Rome died too.
Then did robbers enter Britain from across the Northern
  main
And our Lower River-field was won by Ogier the Dane.

Well could Ogier work his war-boat – well could Ogier
  wield his brand –
Much he knew of foaming waters – not so much of
  farming land.
So he called to him a Hobden of the old unaltered blood,
Saying: 'What about that River-piece; she doesn't look no
  good?'

And that aged Hobden answered: ' 'Tain't for *me* to
  interfere,
But I've known that bit o' meadow now for five and fifty
  year.
Have it *jest* as you've a mind to, but I've proved it time
  on time,
If you want to change her nature you have *got* to give her lime!'

Ogier sent his wains to Lewes, twenty hours' solemn walk,
And drew back great abundance of the cool, grey healing chalk.
And old Hobden spread it broadcast, never heeding what was in't. –
Which is why in cleaning ditches, now and then we find a flint.

Ogier died. His sons grew English – Anglo-Saxon was their name –
Till out of blossomed Normandy another pirate came;
For Duke William conquered England and divided with his men,
And our Lower River-field he gave to William of Warenne.

But the Brook (you know her habit) rose one rainy autumn night
And tore down sodden flitches of the bank to left and right.
So, said William to his Bailiff as they rode their dripping rounds:
'Hob, what about that River-bit – the Brook's got up no bounds?'

And that aged Hobden answered: ' 'Tain't my business to advise,
But ye might ha' known 'twould happen from the way the valley lies.
Where he can't hold back the water you must try and save the sile.
Hev it jest as you've a *mind* to, but, if I was you, I'd spile!'

They spiled along the water-course with trunks of willow-
trees,
And planks of elms behind 'em and immortal oaken
knees.
And when the spates of Autumn whirl the gravel-beds
away
You can see their faithful fragments, iron-hard in iron
clay.

Georgii Quinti Anno Sexto, I, who own the River-field,
Am fortified with title-deeds, attested, signed and sealed,
Guaranteeing me, my assigns, my executors and heirs
All sorts of powers and profits which – are neither mine
nor theirs.

I have rights of chase and warren, as my dignity requires.
I can fish – but Hobden tickles. I can shoot – but
Hobden wires.
I repair, but he reopens, certain gaps which, men allege,
Have been used by every Hobden since a Hobden
swapped a hedge.

Shall I dog his morning progress o'er the track-betraying
dew?
Demand his dinner-basket into which my pheasant flew?
Confiscate his evening faggot under which my conies ran,
And summons him to judgment? I would sooner
summons Pan.

His dead are in the churchyard – thirty generations laid.
Their names were old in history when Domesday Book
was made;
And the passion and the piety and prowess of his line
Have seeded, rooted, fruited in some land the Law calls
mine.

Nor for any beast that burrows, nor for any bird that
flies,
Would I lose his large sound counsel, miss his keen
amending eyes.
He is bailiff, woodman, wheelwright, field-surveyor,
engineer,
And if flagrantly a poacher – 'tain't for me to interfere.

'Hob, what about that River-bit?' I turn to him again,
With Fabricius and Ogier and William of Warenne.
'Hev it jest as you've a mind to, *but*' – and here he takes
command.
For whoever pays the taxes old Mus' Hobden owns the
land.

A DIVERSITY OF CREATURES

ONE WAS a journeyman bricklayer who, I remember, kept a store of gold sovereigns loose in his pocket, and kindly built us a wall; but so leisurely that he came to be almost part of the establishment. When we wished to sink a well opposite some cottages, he said he had the gift of water-finding, and I testify that, when he held one fork of the hazel Y and I the other, the thing bowed itself against all the grip of my hand over an unfailing supply.

Then, out of the woods that know everything and tell nothing, came two dark and mysterious Primitives. They had heard. They would sink that well, for they had the 'gift.' Their tools were an enormous wooden trug, a portable windlass whose handles were curved, and smooth as ox-horns, and a short-handled hoe. They made a ring of brickwork on the bare ground and, with their hands at first, grubbed out the dirt beneath it. As the ring sank they heightened it, course by course, grubbing out with the hoe, till the shaft, true as a rifle-barrel, was deep enough to call for their Father of Trugs, which one brother down below would fill, and the other haul up on the magic windlass. When we stopped, at twenty-five feet, we had found a Jacobean tobacco-pipe, a worn Cromwellian latten spoon and, at the bottom of all, the bronze cheek of a Roman horse-bit.

In cleaning out an old pond which might have been an ancient marl-pit or mine-head, we dredged two intact Elizabethan 'sealed quarts' that Christopher Sly affected, all pearly with the patina of centuries. Its deepest mud yielded us a perfectly polished Neolithic axe-head with but one chip on its still venomous edge.

SOMETHING OF MYSELF

JUST at dusk, a soft September rain began to fall on the hop-pickers. The mothers wheeled the bouncing perambulators out of the gardens; bins were put away, and tally-books made up. The young couples strolled home, two to each umbrella, and the single men walked behind them laughing. Dan and Una, who had been picking after their lessons, marched off to roast poatoes at the oast-house, where old Hobden, with Blue-eyed Bess, his lurcher dog, lived all the month through, drying the hops.

They settled themselves, as usual, on the sack-strewn cot in front of the fires, and, when Hobden drew up the shutter, stared, as usual, at the flameless bed of coals spouting its heat up the dark well of the old-fashioned roundel. Slowly he cracked off a few fresh pieces of coal, packed them, with fingers that never flinched, exactly where they would do most good; slowly he reached behind him till Dan tilted the potatoes into his iron scoop of a hand; carefully he arranged them round the fire, and then stood for a moment, black against the glare. As he

closed the shutter, the oast-house seemed dark before the day's end, and he lit the candle in the lanthorn.

The children heard their shovels rasp on the cloth where the yellow hops lie drying above the fires, and all the oast-house filled with the sweet, sleepy smell as they were turned.

'Who is it?' Una whispered to the Bee Boy.

'Dunno, no more'n you – if *you* dunno,' said he, and smiled.

The voices on the drying-floor talked and chuckled together, and the heavy footsteps moved back and forth. Presently a hop-pocket dropped through the press-hole overhead, and stiffened and fattened as they shovelled it full. 'Clank!' went the press, and rammed the loose stuff into tight cake.

'Gently!' they heard Hobden cry. 'You'll bust her crop if you lay on so. You be as careless as Gleason's bull, Tom. Come an' sit by the fires. She'll do now.'

They came down, and Hobden opened the shutter to see if the potatoes were done.

DYMCHURCH FLIT

Old Mother Laidinwool

(Enlarged from Old Song)

OLD MOTHER Laidinwool had nigh twelve months been dead.
She heard the hops was doing well, an' so popped up her head,
For said she: 'The lads I've picked with when I was young and fair,
They're bound to be at hopping and I'm bound to meet 'em there!'

Let me up and go
Back to the work I know, Lord!
Back to the work I know, Lord!
For it's dark where I lie down, My Lord!
An' it's dark where I lie down!

Old Mother Laidinwool, she give her bones a shake,
An' trotted down the churchyard-path as fast as she could make.
She met the Parson walking, but she says to him, says she:–
'Oh, don't let no one trouble for a poor old ghost like me!'

'Twas all a warm September an' the hops had flourished grand.
She saw the folks get into 'em with stockin's on their hands;
An' none of 'em was foreigners but all which she had known,
And old Mother Laidinwool she blessed 'em every one.

She saw her daughters picking an' their children them-
beside,
An' she moved among the babies an' she stilled 'em when
they cried.
She saw their clothes was bought, not begged, an' they
was clean an' fat,
An' Old Mother Laidinwool she thanked the Lord for
that.

Old Mother Laidinwool she waited on all day
Until it come too dark to see an' people went away –
Until it come too dark to see an' lights began to show,
An' old Mother Laidinwool she hadn't where to go.

Old Mother Laidinwool she give her bones a shake,
An' trotted back to churchyard-mould as fast as she
could make.
She went where she was bidden to an' there laid down
her ghost, . . .
An' the Lord have mercy on you in the Day you need it
most!

Let me in again,
Out of the wet an' rain, Lord!
Out of the wet an' rain, Lord!
For it's best as You shall say, My Lord!
An' it's best as You shall say!

COLLECTED VERSE

IT WAS too hot to run about in the open, so Dan asked their friend, old Hobden, to take their own dinghy from the pond and put her on the brook at the bottom of the garden. Her painted name was the *Daisy*, but for exploring expeditions she was the *Golden Hind* or the *Long Serpent*, or some such suitable name. Dan hiked and howked with a boat-hook (the brook was too narrow for sculls), and Una punted with a piece of hop-pole. When they came to a very shallow place (the *Golden Hind* drew quite three inches of water) they disembarked and scuffled her over the gravel by her tow-rope, and when they reached the overgrown banks beyond the garden they pulled themselves up stream by the low branches.

That day they intended to discover the North Cape like 'Othere, the old sea-captain,' in the book of verses which Una had brought with her; but on account of the heat they changed it to a voyage up the Amazon and the sources of the Nile. Even on the shaded water the air was hot and heavy with drowsy scents, while outside, through breaks in the trees, the sunshine burned the pasture like fire. The kingfisher was asleep on his watching-branch, and the blackbirds scarcely took the trouble to dive into the next bush. Dragon-flies wheeling and clashing were the only things at work, except the moorhens and a big Red Admiral, who flapped down out of the sunshine for a drink.

When they reached Otter Pool the *Golden Hind* grounded comfortably on a shallow, and they lay beneath a roof of close green, watching the water trickle over the flood-gates down the mossy brick chute from the mill-stream to the brook. A big trout – the children knew him well – rolled head and shoulder at some fly that sailed round the bend, while once in just so often the brook rose a fraction of an inch against all the wet pebbles, and they watched the slow draw and shiver of a breath of air through the tree-tops. Then the little voices of the slipping water began again.

'It's like the shadows talking, isn't it?' said Una.

THE KNIGHTS OF THE JOYOUS VENTURE

'Our Fathers of Old'

EXCELLENT herbs had our fathers of old –
Excellent herbs to ease their pain –
Alexanders and Marigold,
  Eyebright, Orris, and Elecampane –
Basil, Rocket, Valerian, Rue,
  (Almost singing themselves they run)
Vervain, Dittany, Call-me-to-you –
  Cowslip, Melilot, Rose of the Sun.
    Anything green that grew out of the mould
    Was an excellent herb to our fathers of old.

Wonderful tales had our fathers of old,
  Wonderful tales of the herbs and the stars –
The Sun was Lord of the Marigold,
  Basil and Rocket belonged to Mars.
Pat as a sum in division it goes –
  (Every herb had a planet bespoke) –
Who but Venus should govern the Rose?
  Who but Jupiter own the Oak?
    Simply and gravely the facts are told
    In the wonderful books of our fathers of old.

Wonderful little, when all is said,
  Wonderful little our fathers knew.
Half their remedies cured you dead –
  Most of their teaching was quite untrue –
'Look at the stars when a patient is ill
  (Dirt has nothing to do with disease),
Bleed and blister as much as you will
  Blister and bleed him as oft as you please.'
    Whence enormous and manifold
    Errors were made by our fathers of old.

Yet when the sickness was sore in the land,
   And neither planets nor herbs assuaged,
They took their lives in their lancet-hand
   And, oh, what a wonderful war they waged!
Yes, when the crosses were chalked on the door –
   (Yes, when the terrible dead-cart rolled!)
Excellent courage our fathers bore –
   Excellent heart had our fathers of old.
      None too learned, but nobly bold
      Into the fight went our fathers of old.

If it be certain, as Galen says –
   And sage Hippocrates holds as much –
'That those afflicted by doubts and dismays
   Are mightily helped by a dead man's touch,'
Then, be good to us, stars above!
   Then, be good to us, herbs below!
We are afflicted by what we can prove,
   We are distracted by what we know.
            So – ah, so!
      Down from your heaven or up from your mould,
      Send us the hearts of our fathers of old!

REWARDS AND FAIRIES

THEY were fishing, a few days later, in the bed of the brook that for centuries had cut deep into the soft valley soil. The trees closing overhead made long tunnels through which the sunshine worked in blobs and patches. Down in the tunnels were bars of sand and gravel, old roots and trunks covered with moss or painted red by the irony water; foxgloves growing lean and pale towards the light; clumps of fern and thirsty shy flowers who could not live away from moisture and shade. In the pools you could see the wave thrown up by the trouts as they charged hither and yon, and the pools were joined to each other – except in flood time, when all was one brown rush – by sheets of thin broken water that poured themselves chuckling round the darkness of the next bend.

YOUNG MEN AT THE MANOR

The Recall

I AM the land of their fathers.
In me the virtue stays.
I will bring back my children,
After certain days.

Under their feet in the grasses
My clinging magic runs.
They shall return as strangers,
They shall remain as sons.

Over their heads in the branches
Of their new-bought, ancient trees,
I weave an incantation
And draw them to my knees.

Scent of smoke in the evening,
Smell of rain in the night –
The hours, the days and the seasons,
Order their souls aright,

Till I make plain the meaning
Of all my thousand years –
Till I fill their hearts with knowledge,
While I fill their eyes with tears.

ACTIONS AND REACTIONS

'Very Many People'

ON THE Downs, in the Weald, on the Marshes,
I heard the Old Gods say:
'Here come Very Many People:
'We must go away.

'They take our land to delight in,
'But their delight destroys.
'They flay the turf from the sheep-walk.
'They load the Denes with noise.

'They burn coal in the woodland.
'They seize the oast and the mill.
'They camp beside Our dew-ponds.
'They mar the clean-flanked hill.

'They string a clamorous Magic
'To fence their souls from thought,
'Till Our deep-breathed Oaks are silent,
'And Our muttering Downs tell nought.

'They comfort themselves with neighbours.
'They cannot bide alone.
'I shall be best for their doings
'When We Old Gods are gone.'

Farewell to the Downs and the Marshes,
And the Weald and the Forest known
Before there were Very Many People,
And the Old Gods had gone!

COLLECTED VERSE

Index

Alnascher and the Oxen *Debits and Credits* 14
Charm, A *Rewards and Fairies* 29
Cuckoo Song *Collected Verse* 30
Eddi's Service *Rewards and Fairies* 21
Flight, The *Collected Verse* 20
Land, The *Diversity of Creatures* 40
Norman and Saxon *Collected Verse* 36
Old Mother Laidinwool *Collected Verse* 46
Our Fathers of Old *Rewards and Fairies* 50
Puck's Song *Puck of Pook's Hill* 8
Recall, The *Actions and Reactions* 53
Run of the Downs *Rewards and Fairies* 26
Smugglers' Song, A *Puck of Pook's Hill* 18
Sussex *Collected Verse* 24
Three Part Song, A *Puck of Pook's Hill* 7
The Way Through The Woods *Rewards and Fairies* 13
Tree Song, A *Puck of Pook's Hill* 35
'Very Many People' *Collected Verse* 54

'Have you ever bin in the marsh?' *Dymchurch Flit, Puck of Pook's Hill* 17
It was too hot to run about in the open
Knights of the Joyous Venture, Puck of Pook's Hill 48
Just at dusk, a soft September rain *Dymchurch Flit, Puck of Pook's Hill* 44
Just beyond the west fringe of our land *Something of Myself* 12
One view called me to another *They, Traffics and Discoveries* 27
One was a journeyman bricklayer *Something of Myself* 43
The children went to the seaside
The Knife and the Naked Chalk, Rewards and Fairies 31
Then they walked through the grass *Hal O' the Draft, Puck of Pook's Hill* 10
The new church visitor *The Wish House, Debits and Credits* 22
There came at last a brilliant day *They, Traffics and Discoveries* 28
The valley was choked with fog *Friendly Brook, Diversity of Creatures* 38
They were fishing a few days later
Young Men at the Manor, Puck of Pook's Hill 52

Colour illustrations

North of Ninfield Title page
Batemans 4
Ypres Tower, Rye 9
Long Slip Meadow 12
Mount Caburn 25
Sea Fog Rising 28
Spear Thistle 29
Weir on the Dudwell 41
Wealden Oasts 45
Otter Pool 49
Pevensey Levels 53

Wood-engravings

Chalk Quarry near Ringmer 7
The Gunway 13
Beached Fishing Boats 17
Stopham Bridge 27
Southdown Sheep 31
Winter Thorn 35
Ypres Tower, Rye 56

THE ARTIST'S EYE
VICTOR PASMORE

An exhibition of National Gallery paintings
selected by the artist

Commentary by Victor Pasmore

The National Gallery, London
4 July – 7 October 1990

Sponsored by Marlborough Fine Art

First published in Great Britain in 1990 by National Gallery Publications Limited
5/6 Pall Mall East, London SW1Y 5BA

British Library Cataloguing in Publication Data
National Gallery, Great Britain
The artist's eye – Victor Pasmore: an exhibition of National Gallery paintings selected by the artist: the National Gallery, London 4 July–7 October 1990. – (Artist's eye exhibitions).
1. European paintings – Catalogues, indexes
I. Title II. Pasmore, Victor, *1908–* III. Series
759.94074

ISBN 0–947645–76–4

Designed by Joe Swift
Typeset by Wyvern Typesetting Ltd, Bristol
Printed and bound in Great Britain by White Dove Press Ltd

Front cover: *Still Life* (detail), by Jan van de Velde.
Back cover: *Living Water*, by Victor Pasmore.

Sponsor's Foreword

The Directors of Marlborough Fine Art are delighted to be involved in the sponsorship of the excellent series 'The Artist's Eye' at the National Gallery. These exhibitions have always proved stimulating and enlightening in the past and Victor Pasmore's selection continues this tradition.

The Duke of Beaufort, Chairman
Marlborough Fine Art

Foreword

In 1982, Victor Pasmore was made a Companion of Honour by Her Majesty The Queen, in recognition of his great contribution to the art of this century, and we are delighted that he has consented to select our tenth 'Artist's Eye' exhibition. Pasmore occupies the enviable position of a senior revolutionary and his views on the National Gallery Collection, as progressing from one revolution in seeing and painting to another, have a coherence that could not be derived from a solely scholarly starting point. Once again, 'The Artist's Eye' presents to the public their pictures in a sequence that cuts across the tidy and familiar curatorial arrangements. This is a personal interpretation of the European tradition and also very much the view of an insider, of someone who played an active role in that 'modern revolution' to which Pasmore refers in his introduction, working alongside and exchanging ideas with, among others, Picasso, Moore, Hepworth and Nicholson.

The opinion that recurs most often in Pasmore's commentary on the paintings he has selected is one formulated by an artist used to creating abstract, 'independent' works of art. It is that the great works of the past are themselves 'independent', that is to say, they communicate themselves to us not through any specific meaning or symbolism that they may have held for their own times, but through their intrinsic, subjective, and ultimately 'independent' spirit.

This is a reinterpretation of the past by an artist of a particularly significant generation, a reinterpretation whose validity encourages all of us to understand and respond to these great works of art on our own terms. And for this we must be grateful to Victor Pasmore for lending us his 'eye'.

Our gratitude goes also to Marlborough Fine Art (London) Ltd for generously supporting this exhibition and making it possible.

I must add, too, particular thanks to my colleague Colin Wiggins who has worked with Victor Pasmore on the exhibition and the catalogue, and contributed so much to their success.

Neil MacGregor, Director

The Renaissance and the Modern Revolution of Painting

For an artist who claims to be involved in the modern revolution of painting, an invitation to select a choice of pictures from the National Gallery Collection offers a challenge, particularly when it is a condition that he include an example of his own work.

The fact that the National Gallery starts its Collection with the Italian Renaissance means that it begins with a previous revolution in which visual naturalism replaced subjective formalism in the representation of religious symbols. But the naturalism of Renaissance painting, even in its most religious form, was essentially an extraneous affair; nature seen and conceived objectively from the outside like the image in a mirror. Indeed the mirror, together with the sciences of anatomy and perspective, became the objective criteria of naturalist painting until its 'mirror image' was mechanised by the invention of photography.

The challenge of the photograph was followed by that of revolutionary developments in science and natural philosophy. In contrast to the measurable world of the Renaissance and classical science the modern world presents a process of opposing forces, evolutionary developments and ambiguous relationships. Attempts to rationalise this in philosophy have been echoed in the abstract, conceptual and ambiguous imagery of modern art. In contrast to the Renaissance, therefore, modern painting is the product of a subjective revolution.

To meet these challenges painting had to become experimental and independent; hence its unprecedented diversity and individuality. The first experiments, Fauvism and Cubism, tackled the problem of the ambiguous relationship between objective and subjective reality. By fragmenting the visual object and rearranging its parts as an independent pictorial image, a synthesis was achieved between objective representation and subjective freedom. But the increase in pictorial independence which this process involved led to a further experiment – abstract art – which rejected visual representation altogether and developed the painting as a completely independent object. Later all this was countered by the Surrealists who, after accusing the Cubists of destroying the visual object, retained its traditional image but in terms of 'surreal' or paradoxical relationships.

Fragmentation enabled the painter to symbolise the relativity of perception as well as the new multi-dimensional concept of space, but it did so at the expense of the objects represented. But while Cubism destroyed the visual object, Surrealism destroyed the Cubist dynamic image. As a result, modern painting split in two: one half – Fauvism, Cubism and their derivatives – maintained visual representation but with increased and diverse forms of independence; the other half – abstract art – demanded the complete autonomy of painting as an independent object analogous to music.

Historically and socially the implications of the modern revolution may be more far-reaching in the sense that they are symptomatic of a new emanation of the human spirit in the twentieth century, which has found expression not only in unprecedented social, scientific and technical advances, but also in the terrible tragedies that man has brought upon himself in our time.

Basically, painting is a language about visual objects expressed in terms of subjective effect – that is to say their beauty. But what is the function of beauty in relation to man and the natural world, and why can the world appear beautiful in its most violent as well as its most peaceful forms? In the past, religious painting provided a link between sensibility and the mystery of God, but now the link is with Nature. What is the reality of the sky without the beauty of the stars spread across the surface of the night? To be told that the stars are only objects leads us further away rather than nearer the mystery of their existence.

Victor Pasmore

Victor Pasmore

VICTOR PASMORE, Living Water, 1990

PIERO DELLA FRANCESCA

active 1439; died 1492

The Baptism of Christ

The rediscovery of Piero is a relatively recent development dating from the late nineteenth century, and was initiated mainly by Charles Blanc, Director of the Ecole des Beaux-Arts in Paris, where Seurat was a student. For Seurat, Piero offered the possibility of creating a new kind of classicism, based on Impressionism.

However, the classicism of Piero, unlike that of Uccello, is not abstract. In *The Baptism of Christ*, not only are the figures individual and human, but the landscape in which they are set, with its light, space and colour, is full of sentiment and personal sensibility. Moreover, odd surprises, such as the man removing his shirt, transform what could have been a purely academic exercise into a romantic and personal image.

Fig. 1 Seurat, *Bathers at Asnières*.

10

PAOLO UCCELLO
about 1397–1475

The Battle of San Romano

It was said of Uccello that after being told about the new science of perspective, he could think and talk of nothing else. As a result he created this painting, of pure conception.

'I hope I shall come to express with great precision', wrote the Cubist Juan Gris, 'a reality imagined in terms of pure intellectual elements . . . an object can be looked at in innumerable ways. For a painter it will be simply a grouping of flat coloured forms.' Uccello's remarkable painting, therefore, can be regarded as a precursor of Cubism.

Fig. 2 Juan Gris, *The Glass*.

SANDRO BOTTICELLI
about 1445–1510

'Mystic Nativity'

In this painting the Renaissance revival of pagan mythology has been rejected in favour of a reaffirmation of Christian belief, represented with naturalism, sentiment and childlike simplicity, but nevertheless saturated with esoteric symbols.

It seems that Botticelli was deeply affected by the powerful and fanatical Christian fundamentalist and preacher, Savonarola, and subsequently renounced the paganism of his most famous paintings, such as the *Venus and Mars*, also in the National Gallery.

The most attractive explanation of this picture is that it embodies an omen for peace during troubled and murderous times in Florence. Whatever its meaning, the painting stands today as a masterpiece in the great tradition of independent painting, firmly attached to reality and impregnated with a unique personal aesthetic.

LEONARDO DA VINCI

1452–1519

The Virgin of the Rocks

'To bathe objects in light is to merge them with the infinite.' Here, in one short and beautiful sentence, is condensed the whole of Leonardo's remarkable thought, poetic sensibility and unique visual aesthetic. Things seen in the light of science, but their image in art illuminated by their spirit.

This antithetical relationship seems to be inherent not only in the aesthetic, but also in the symbolism of his later work. For instance, the physical connection between the Virgin and her mother, Saint Anne, in the *Cartoon* in the National Gallery seems to be deliberately ambiguous – partly separate and partly joined; while the relationship between the 'angel' and the Virgin in this picture – each with a similar child – also seems enigmatic.

This ambiguity in relationship suggests that both pictures were intended to have two meanings, one conventional and the other secret. For instance, Leonardo may have been attracted to the mystic heresy that there were two Virgins and two Jesus children, one spiritual and the other earthly, a condition subconsciously similar to his own dual personality – that of imaginative artist and empirical scientist.

Fig. 3 Leonardo da Vinci, *Cartoon* (detail).

However, be that as it may, the symbolic meaning of both pictures belongs to the past, but the enigma created by Leonardo's unique visual aesthetic belongs eternally to the present.

TITIAN
active before 1511; died 1576
The Death of Actaeon

This late painting by Titian can be compared to El Greco's *Christ driving the Traders from the Temple* in the sense that it is not only expressionist in form – that is to say, distorted – but also impressionist because it is concerned more with the diffusion of form in space by light than with its objective delineation, as in the work of Michelangelo. It is this subjective distortion that has given the late works by Titian and El Greco a special interest for modern artists.

The composition of this painting, like that of the El Greco, has an objective independence which is also in itself expressive of the drama and tragedy of the scene.

EL GRECO
1541–1614

Christ driving the Traders from the Temple

In the famous treatise on painting (*Della Pittura*, 1436) by the Renaissance artist and scholar Alberti, geometry is fundamental to all painting as a means of conveying its spatial representation and perspective, as well as forming the composition and partitioning of the picture plane. More important, however, was what Alberti called the *Istoria*, by which he means the narrative, with its dramatic and emotional content.

The separation of geometry and *Istoria* into two different chapters of the treatise may have been the reason for their separation in subsequent academic teaching, with the result that many artists fell into the trap of concentrating too much on one at the expense of the other.

However, *Christ driving the Traders from the Temple*, like Titian's *Death of Actaeon*, is a superb example in which the two elements are completely integrated; that is to say, in which the pictorial composition directly and independently expresses the emotional content.

Fig. 4 Titian, *The Death of Actaeon*.

CLAUDE
1600–1682
Landscape with Narcissus and Echo

With painting achieving increasing independence from the patronage of the Church, naturalism began to take on a new significance, with a new God, 'Nature', and a new symbol 'landscape'. During the Renaissance, landscape had served only as the background to religious and secular narratives, but by the seventeenth century it had begun to achieve independence, representing nature in two ways. There was the empirical way, initiated by Dutch painters such as Ruisdael, Rembrandt and Hobbema (to be followed later in England by Constable, and in France by Courbet and the Impressionists), and there was the purely logical, conceptual and idealistic way of classical art, as illustrated in the works of Claude and Poussin.

Fig. 5 Poussin, *Landscape with Man killed by a Snake*.

JAN VAN DE VELDE
1620–1662 or later

Still Life

This little picture is one of the supreme masterpieces in this selection of paintings, but the question arises as to how a work depicting only a glass jar, two halves of a lemon, and a knife can be compared with paintings of human and religious content such as those in this exhibition.

The real content of this painting is not the jar or the lemon or the knife, but the subjective spirit of the artist, which, in the final analysis, is the real content of all great painting. Indeed, it is for this reason that the painting of still life has been one of the main sources of inspiration in modern painting, from Cézanne and Van Gogh to Braque and Picasso.

It is true, of course, that religious, social and human content can engage the mind and extend the imagination to a far greater degree than a still life. But while there are thousands of religious and human paintings which engage the mind and stimulate the imagination, only a very few have the supreme subjective qualities required of great art. This still life, on the other hand, may be only a fragment of objective experience, but its subjective content is total and absolute.

Fig. 6 Picasso, *Fruit Dish, Bottle and Violin*.

REMBRANDT
1606–1669
Margaretha de Geer

Rembrandt's place within the context of the naturalist tradition presents a dichotomy resembling that of Leonardo – empirical realism on the one hand and, on the other, theological naturalism. For Rembrandt, nature belonged to God, whose presence shines out of the centre of things so that objects are not only bathed in scientific light, but also illuminated from within.

As with Leonardo this dichotomy forms the basis of Rembrandt's unique visual aesthetic, expressed as a completely independent pictorial image.

Fig. 7 Rembrandt, *The Jewish Bride*.

JACOB VAN RUISDAEL
1628/9–1682

A Pool surrounded by Trees

This great landscape painting by Ruisdael was painted one hundred and fifty years before Constable's *Hay Wain* and Turner's *Frosty Morning*. Its empirical approach can be considered as anticipating the main developments in much nineteenth-century English and French painting.

Fig. 8 Turner, *Frosty Morning*.

JOHN CONSTABLE
1776–1837

The Hay Wain

In spite of its academic, geometric composition and conventional adherence to the science of perspective, *The Hay Wain* must be counted as one of the great masterpieces of naturalist painting.

The main problem posed by the naturalist tradition was that it forced the painter to walk a tightrope not only between a subjective vision of the scene and an objective knowledge of it, but also between the reality of the visual object and that of the painting itself. Somehow, by a process of pure sensibility, Constable managed to reconcile these opposing conditions. Constable often made two versions of his major landscapes – first a full-sized sketch, closely based on direct observation from nature, and finally a conceptual development adapted to the principles of classical art.

The Hay Wain, therefore, represents a link between the objective and idealist concepts of classical landscape painting and the later subjective and empirical vision of the French Impressionists.

Fig. 9 Constable, sketch for *Leaping Horse*.

JOSEPH MALLORD WILLIAM TURNER
1775–1851

Margate(?) from the Sea

'If Turner could make a selection of his work today', wrote Walter Sickert, 'he could still claim to be the first of the moderns.'

The modern revolution of painting had its origins in Paris, first through Impressionism, Post-Impressionism and Symbolism in the late nineteenth century and subsequently through Fauvism and Cubism in the twentieth. While this is true in a collective sense, it can be claimed that Constable was a dynamic impressionist long before Monet, and Turner a militant post-impressionist before Cézanne and the Cubists.

By changing the content of painting from the perception of landscape illuminated from the outside, to the idea of landscape diffused and absorbed in the colour of light, Turner anticipated the Cubists by arriving at a world of ideas that could not be depicted by visual abstraction. Just as the fragmentation of Cubist form had no visible identity so Turner's fragmentation of light into a composite of colours similarly had no visible reality.

Long before Seurat and the Pointillists had adopted the new science of colour, as a property of light and not of objects, Turner had done likewise in the mid-1830s with such works as *Interior at Petworth*. The unprecedented independence of all his late paintings, both as subjective concepts and as pictorial objects, preceded the revolutionary independence achieved by the Cubists by over seventy years.

Sickert was right, therefore, in his claim that Turner was the first of the moderns.

JEAN-AUGUSTE-DOMINIQUE INGRES
1780–1867

Madame Moitessier

'Supposing the moderns are wrong' replied Ingres to his critics. But the position of Ingres in relation to the modern revolution of painting is ambiguous. On the one hand, he was a militant idealist and Neoclassical reactionary, but on the other a subjective romantic, sensual realist and independent painter. Indeed, his greatest paintings, like *La Grande Odalisque* in the Louvre and this portrait, possess all the autonomy of modern art.

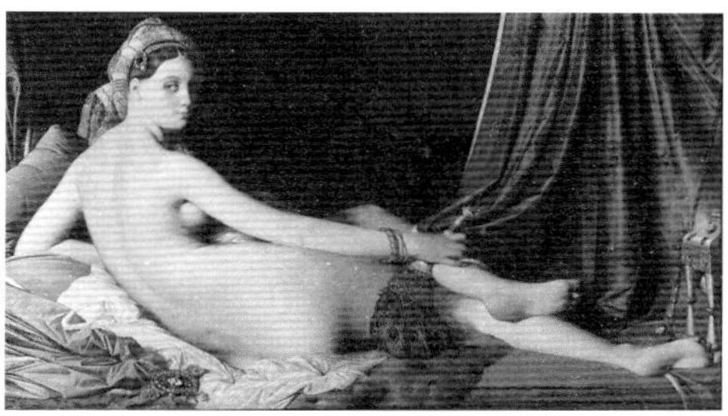

Fig. 10 Ingres, *La Grande Odalisque*.

Me Inès Moitessier
née de Foucauld.

JEAN-FRANCOIS MILLET
1814–1875
The Winnower

Like Leonardo, Millet saw in the landscape of the earth and its toiling peasant labourers an image of the infinite. Millet's religious sentiment was not an empty dream, but was based on the solid rock of the natural earth, which he was able to express in terms of remarkable pictorial independence – as can be seen in this superbly constructed peasant figure. It is perhaps for this reason that Millet was one of Van Gogh's favourite painters.

Fig. 11 Van Gogh, *The Potato Eaters*.

GUSTAVE COURBET
1819–1877

Girls on the Bank of the Seine

Although this picture is only a sketch for one of his major works, no representative selection of European painting would be complete without Courbet, one of the supreme painters of the nineteenth century, who propagated a philosophy of art which gave his work both a moral and a revolutionary aspect. For Courbet, art was both a social responsibility and an individual creative process, opposing approaches which he symbolised in his huge painting in the Musée d'Orsay, *The Studio*, in which he depicted himself surrounded by society while painting an independent image of a landscape. Courbet, therefore, was both a political socialist and an artistic individualist; a dichotomy he was able to maintain through his close friendship with the anarchist and social philosopher, Pierre Joseph Proudhon.

Fig. 12 Picasso, *Les Demoiselles des Bords de la Seine.*

But of course there was something else. 'Courbet', wrote the Surrealist painter Giorgio de Chirico, 'was both a worker and a poet. Romantic, a curious word full of meaning and the far away dream. But for us it means only art that is felt and inspires feeling; and moreover an art that is firmly based on the solid rock of reality.' But it was not only Courbet's romantic poetry that inspired the moderns, it was also his persistent demands, in the face of State opposition, for complete individual independence in painting; a demand which later inspired the modern anarchist, Pablo Picasso, to create one of his finest and most revolutionary paintings in the form of a copy, or rather free interpretation of Courbet's final version of this painting (in the Musée d'Orsay).

JAMES ABBOTT McNEILL WHISTLER
1834–1903

Miss Cicely Alexander

'Why should I not call my works "symphonies", "arrangements", "harmonies" and "nocturnes"? Art should be independent of all clap-trap', wrote Whistler in the 1890s.

The importance of Whistler as one of the major initiators of the modern revolution in painting tends to be underestimated, possibly because, unlike his twentieth-century counterparts, his art is too much of a relic of aristocratic refinement.

'Now, Mr Whistler, can you tell me how long it took to knock off that nocturne?' asked the Attorney General in the famous libel trial with Ruskin. 'About a day' was the reply. So, when his revolutionary ideas forced his resignation as President of the Royal Society of British Artists, Whistler could only comment that 'the artists have gone and the British remain'.

The point is that Whistler was the only painter in England able to follow up the revolutionary independence of Turner. It was not until 1912 that the Vorticists, in London, took up the challenge, but the inspiration this time came via Paris.

Fig. 13 Whistler, *Nocturne in Blue and Silver: Cremorne Lights*.

EDOUARD MANET
1832–1883

The Waitress

This superb, apparently spontaneous painting, as fresh today as when it was painted, combining control and a unique visual aesthetic, is one of the rare, great masterpieces by Manet, and is comparable to his *Olympia*, in the Musée d'Orsay.

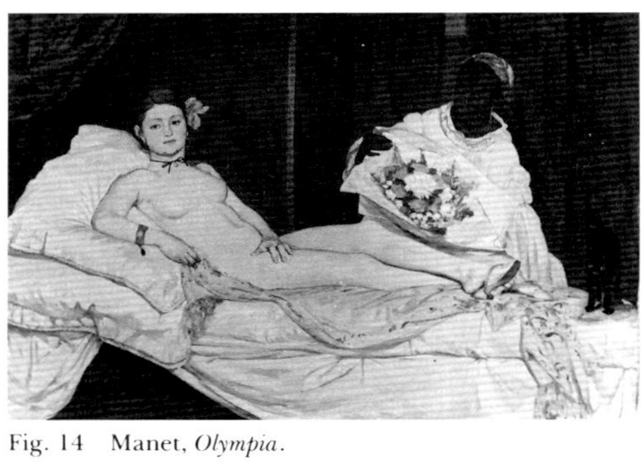

Fig. 14 Manet, *Olympia*.

GEORGES-PIERRE SEURAT
1859–1891

Bathers at Asnières

What is unique and remarkable about this picture, a great masterpiece in the Renaissance tradition of painting, is that it was painted when Seurat was only twenty-three years old, an age at which the average artist, however skilful, is still an immature student.

One explanation of this extraordinary achievement may be that it was the work of two people – on the one hand, Seurat himself, the unique artist who created the visual image, and, on the other, his teacher at the Ecole des Beaux-Arts, Charles Blanc, who provided the intellectual maturity.

Blanc was an exceptionally erudite teacher and academician as well as author of a famous treatise on painting. What links him directly to this painting is his revival of Piero della Francesca, from whose work *Bathers at Asnières* surely drew its supreme inspiration.

Cézanne said that his own aim was to do Poussin again from nature. So it might be claimed that Seurat is here repeating Piero in terms of Impressionism.

Fig. 15 Piero della Francesca, *The Baptism of Christ*.

PAUL CEZANNE
1839–1906
Mountains in Provence

'What interests me', wrote Picasso, 'is the anxiety of Cézanne and the torment of Van Gogh; the rest is unimportant.' In comparing Cézanne with Van Gogh Picasso seems to have been affected by the ambiguous ideas which gripped the scientific and philosophical world at the turn of the twentieth century. What had previously been stable, logical and visible suddenly became volatile and invisible.

The importance of Cézanne is that he was the first painter to be conscious of this new development, and to attempt a pictorial rationalisation of it. 'Everything we see melts away', he wrote, 'but our art must make us feel that it is eternal.'

Fig. 16 Picasso, *'Ma Jolie'*.

Cézanne was also the first to rationalise unequivocally not only the relativity of visual object and observer, but also the autonomous reality of the pictorial image. 'I am the subjective consciousness of the landscape and my canvas is its objective consciousness', he wrote.

The ambiguity involved in this concept forced Cézanne to walk a precarious tightrope between these two opposing realities, a task which he was never able to fulfil to his satisfaction. It is not surprising, therefore, that the Cubist attempt to follow Cézanne's ambiguous dialectic ended in the fragmentation and complete disintegration of the visual object.

VINCENT VAN GOGH
1853–1890

Sunflowers

Picasso's comparison of Van Gogh with Cézanne is interesting because of the fundamental difference in outlook between the two painters. Although both possessed a firmly entrenched empirical vision and an autonomous concept of the pictorial image, Cézanne combined these with an abstract idea of nature. Van Gogh, on the other hand, was drawn by temperament to nature as an expression of individual life.

Whereas Cézanne addressed his art to initiates, Van Gogh aimed to speak to everyone in a simple emotional language. To quote Cézanne, 'Art is a religion and its end is the elevation of thought'; but for Van Gogh, 'I want to say something comforting as music is comforting.'

Van Gogh's individualism and empirical realism were ultimately tested by his confrontation with Gauguin, whose intellectual outlook, like Cézanne's, was basically abstract. Nevertheless, without this influence Van Gogh might not have become both a pioneer of the modern revolution of painting and its supreme popular hero.

Fig. 17 Van Gogh, *Self-Portrait with bandaged Ear*.

It requires both poles of the human psyche, working together in tension, to create great art. 'Why am I so little of an artist that I always regret that the picture is not alive?' writes Van Gogh in one letter; yet in another, 'Colour expresses something in itself. One starts with a hopeless struggle to follow nature. One ends by creating from one's palette and nature agrees.'

Vincent

HENRI ROUSSEAU
1844–1910
Tropical Storm with a Tiger (*Surpris!*)

'I have just put on my twenty-fifth green,' said Rousseau to a friend who had called while he was painting one of his great forest pictures.

This was not the remark of a naive or amateur artist, but that of a highly knowledgeable and sophisticated painter who had spent a lifetime studying painting, not in a school of art but privately, both in his spare time while employed as a customs clerk and then after his retirement. You do not have to go to an art school nowadays to discover the secrets of painting; they can be found on one's own by practice and by constant visits to museums.

Fig. 18 Rousseau, *Negro attacked by a Jaguar*.

A regular exhibitor at the Salon des Indépendants in Paris, where his work frequently caused a sensation, Rousseau was a friend of moderns such as Braque, Apollinaire and Picasso, and deliberately set out to revolutionise painting by subjective methods. 'You and I', he said to the young Picasso, 'are the greatest painters of our time, you in the Egyptian style and I in the modern.'

Rousseau's great forest pictures, such as his *Negro attacked by a Jaguar*, were all painted at the end of his life, between 1906 and 1910. Dated 1891, this painting must have been one of the first inspired versions.

Henri Rousseau

VICTOR PASMORE

A Crime of Ideas, 1989 (after 'The Charnel House' by Picasso)

The modern revolution of painting can be said to have started with the subjective freedom of the Romantic movement, which reached its apogee in England with Turner, and in France with Van Gogh, Gauguin, Cézanne, Seurat and Rousseau, examples of whose work are included in this selection. But, as no major examples of the twentieth-century development of this independence exist in the National Gallery it has been necessary to represent it with a copy of one of its masterpieces.

The Charnel House was painted by Picasso in 1945 during the last year of the war and was intended as a pendant to his famous *Guernica* from the Spanish Civil War. Its imagery was derived from a film showing a family murdered in their kitchen. However, after photographs of the concentration camp at Dachau were published, Picasso identified the scene with the criminal atrocities of the Nazi regime.

So impressed was the art critic Christian Zervos by this second protest and anti-war painting by Picasso that he photographed each stage of its development. The first stages formed a traditional, realistic, objective and three-dimensional representation in terms of expressionist distortion and Picasso's personal style, but drawn only in outline. Finally, the initial drawing was developed into a free, flat and independent painting, with the result that the original unique and dramatic image was destroyed by the patterns of a Cubist-type creation imposed on it.

This copy, or rather free translation, was inspired by the desire to preserve the original image, the loss of which demonstrates the price which had to be paid for the modern demand for subjective independence.

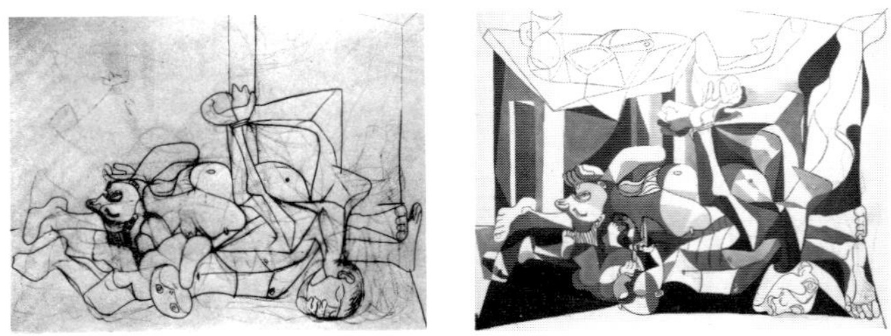

Fig. 19 Picasso, *The Charnel House* (first and final versions).

A CRIME OF IDEAS

Paintings selected by Victor Pasmore

Pages 6–7
Victor Pasmore
Living Water, 1990
Oil on board, 121.9 × 243.8 cm
Marlborough Fine Art (London) Ltd

Page 9
Piero della Francesca (active 1439; died 1492)
The Baptism of Christ
Wood, 167 × 116 cm

Pages 10–11
Paolo Uccello (about 1397–1475)
The Battle of San Romano
Wood, 181.6 × 320 cm

Page 13
Sandro Botticelli (about 1445–1510)
'Mystic Nativity'
Signed and dated 1500(?) in the Greek inscription
Canvas, 108.6 × 74.9 cm

Page 15
Leonardo da Vinci (1452–1519)
The Virgin of the Rocks
Wood, 189.5 × 120 cm

Page 17
Titian (active before 1511; died 1576)
The Death of Actaeon
Canvas, 178.4 × 198.1 cm

Page 19
El Greco (1541–1614)
Christ driving the Traders from the Temple
Canvas, 106.3 × 129.7 cm

Page 21
Claude (1600–1682)
Landscape with Narcissus and Echo
Signed or inscribed, apparently beginning
CLAVDE GILLEE and ending 1644
Canvas, 94.6 × 118.1 cm

Page 23
Jan van de Velde (1620–1662 or later)
Still Life
Signed and dated: Jan·vande·Velde·fecit·An° 1656
Wood, 40.3 × 32.2 cm

Page 25
Rembrandt (1606–1669)
Margaretha de Geer
Canvas, 130.5 × 97.5 cm

Pages 26–7
Jacob van Ruisdael (1628 or 1629(?)–1682)
A Pool surrounded by Trees
Signed, bottom left: JvRuiſdael [JvR in monogram]
Canvas, 107.5 × 143 cm

Pages 28–9
John Constable (1776–1837)
The Hay Wain
Signed and dated: John Constable pinx[t].
London 1821
Canvas, 130.2 × 185.4 cm

Page 31
Joseph Mallord William Turner (1775–1851)
Margate(?) from the Sea
Canvas, 90.2 × 120.7 cm

Page 33
Jean-Auguste-Dominique Ingres (1780–1867)
Madame Moitessier
Signed and dated: J. Jngres 1856/AET LXXVI
Canvas, 120 × 92.1 cm

Page 35
Jean-François Millet (1814–1875)
The Winnower
Signed, bottom left: J. F. Millet
Canvas, 100.5 × 71 cm

Page 37
Jean-Désiré-Gustave Courbet (1819–1877)
Girls on the Bank of the Seine
Canvas, 96.5 × 130 cm

Page 39
James Abbott McNeill Whistler (1834–1903)
Miss Cicely Alexander
Whistler's butterfly signature is on the left
Canvas, 190 × 98 cm

Page 41
Edouard Manet (1832–1883)
The Waitress
Signed and dated: Manet /79(8?)
Canvas, 97.1 × 77.5 cm

Page 42–3
Georges-Pierre Seurat (1859–1891)
Bathers at Asnières
Signed: Seurat
Canvas, 201 × 300 cm

Page 45
Paul Cézanne (1839–1906)
Mountains in Provence
Canvas, 63.5 × 79.4 cm

Page 47
Vincent van Gogh (1853–1890)
Sunflowers
Signed: Vincent
Canvas, 92.1 × 73 cm

Page 49
Henri Rousseau (1844–1910)
Tropical Storm with a Tiger (Surpris!)
Signed and dated: Henri Rousseau, 1891
Canvas, 129.8 × 161 9 cm

Page 51
Victor Pasmore
A Crime of Ideas
(after *The Charnel House* by Picasso), 1989
Charcoal, 152.4 × 167.6 cm
Marlborough Fine Art (London) Ltd

List of Figures

Fig. 1
George-Pierre Seurat (1859–1891)
Bathers at Asnières
201 × 300 cm
The National Gallery, London

Fig. 2
Juan Gris (1887–1927)
The Glass
33 × 18.5 cm
Collection: A. Thurstrup, Duursholm, Sweden
Photo: Galerie Louise Leiris, Paris

Fig. 3
Leonardo da Vinci (1452–1519)
Cartoon: The Virgin and Child with Saint Anne and Saint John the Baptist (detail)
Whole, 141.5 × 104.6 cm
The National Gallery, London

Fig. 4
Titian (active before 1511; died 1576)
The Death of Actaeon
178.4 × 198.1 cm
The National Gallery, London

Fig. 5
Nicolas Poussin (1594?–1665)
Landscape with a Man killed by a Snake
119.4 × 198.8 cm
The National Gallery, London

Fig. 6
Pablo Picasso (1881–1873)
Fruit Dish, Bottle and Violin
92 × 73 cm
The National Gallery, London
© DACS 1990

Fig. 7
Rembrandt (1606–1669)
The Jewish Bride
121.5 × 166.5 cm
Rijksmuseum, Amsterdam

Fig. 8
Joseph Mallord William Turner (1775–1851)
Frosty Morning
113.7 × 174.6 cm
Turner Collection, Tate Gallery, London

Fig. 9
John Constable (1776–1837)
Sketch for *Leaping Horse*
129.4 × 188 cm
Victoria and Albert Museum, London
Photo: Courtesy of the Board of Trustees of the V&A

Fig. 10
Jean-Auguste-Dominique Ingres (1780–1867)
La Grande Odalisque
Musée du Louvre, Paris
Photo: Cliché des Musées Nationaux, Paris

Fig. 11
Vincent van Gogh (1853–1890)
The Potato Eaters
82 × 114 cm
Vincent van Gogh Foundation/National Museum
Vincent van Gogh, Amsterdam

Fig. 12
Pablo Picasso (1881–1973)
Les Demoiselles des Bords de la Seine
100.5 × 201 cm
Oeffentliche Kunstsammlung Basel, Kunstmuseum
© DACS 1990

Fig. 13
James Abbott McNeill Whistler (1834–1903)
Nocturne in Blue and Silver: Cremorne Lights
50.2 × 74.9 cm
Tate Gallery, London

Fig. 14
Edouard Manet (1832–1883)
Olympia
130.5 × 190 cm
Musée d'Orsay, Paris
Photo: Cliché des Musées Nationaux, Paris

Fig. 15
Piero della Francesca (active 1439; died 1492)
The Baptism of Christ
167 × 116 cm
The National Gallery, London

Fig. 16
Pablo Picasso (1881–1973)
'Ma Jolie' Paris (winter 1911–12)
Oil on canvas, 100 × 65.4 cm
Collection, The Museum of Modern Art, New York.
Acquired through the Lillie P. Bliss Bequest.
© DACS 1990

Fig. 17
Vincent van Gogh (1853–1890)
Self-Portrait with bandaged Ear
60 × 49 cm
Courtauld Institute Galleries, London
(Courtauld Collection)

Fig. 18
Henri Rousseau (1844–1910)
Negro attacked by a Jaguar
114 × 162.5 cm
Oeffentliche Kunstsammlung Basel, Kunstmuseum

Fig. 19
Pablo Picasso (1881–1973)
The Charnel House (first state)
199.8 × 250.1 cm
Photo: Cahiers d'Art, Paris
© DACS
The Charnel House Paris (1944–5; dated 1945)
Oil and charcoal on canvas, 199.8 × 250.1 cm
Collection, The Museum of Modern Art, New York.
Mrs Sam A. Lewisohn Bequest (by exchange) and
Mrs Marya Bernard Fund in memory of her husband
Dr Bernard Bernard and anonymous funds.
© DACS 1990

Victor Pasmore

Photo: John Pasmore

1908 Born Chelsham, Surrey.

1925–7 Painted local landscape in impressionist style.

1927–37 Moved to London. Employed in LCC local government service.
Paints during spare time; influenced by Matisse, Picasso and the School of Paris.

1937 Reacts against the School of Paris and returns to traditional painting; opens a teaching studio with William Coldstream and Claude Rogers, later known as the Euston Road School.

1940–7 Marries. Lives by the Thames at Chiswick Mall and paints riverside scenes.

1947 Returns to abstract painting, after seeing Picasso's exhibition of work painted during the war.

1950–1 Joins Ben Nicholson and Barbara Hepworth at the Penwith Society, exhibitions in St Ives, Cornwall.
Organises the first post-war exhibitions of purely abstract art in England.

1959 CBE

1960 Retrospective exhibition, British Pavilion, Venice Biennale, and subsequent European tour.

1963–6 Trustee of the Tate Gallery, London.

1964 Carnegie prize, Pittsburgh International, USA.

1965 Retrospective exhibitions, Tate Gallery, London, São Paulo Biennale and South American Tour.

1977 Grand Prix – Graphics International Biennale, Ljubljana, Yugoslavia.

1980 Retrospective exhibition, Royal Academy of Arts, London.

1982 Created Companion of Honour.

1988 Retrospective exhibition, Yale Center for British Art, and Phillips Collection, Washington DC, USA.